Gunner Gets Lucky

Written by
Karl Riemensperger

To all those dogs, through no fault of their own, who experienced abuse, abandonment or neglect, and who did not find themselves "Lucky" to have been given second chances in life.

Too many dogs are abused, stranded, or owner surrendered and never make it to foster or "furever" homes. For this reason, a portion of the proceeds of this book will benefit Florida All-Retriever Rescue (FARR) – Gunner's ultimate route and destination to his "furever" home!
Florida All Retriever Rescue Dog Rescue Group (flretrieverrescue.org)

Text copyright © 2022 by Karl Riemensperger
Illustrations copyright © 2022 Transcend Studio LLC

First edition
Printed in United States of America
ISBN: 9798843292683

www.gunnergoesseries.com
www.transcendstudio.ninja

Gunner woke from his daily mid-day nap to a commotion of noisy dogs.

Looking directly at Gunner, the old man asked, "Are you ready, Gunner?" as the other dogs slinked off under the porch and hid.

"Ready for what?" Gunner thought to himself, as a big, white van pulled up and a portly man jumped out. Gunner had already spent several weeks getting comfortable at the farmhouse in Alabama with five other dogs. He usually made the best of things and it had just started feeling like home.

The barking and the smell (of 25 or so dogs) poured out of the van when the doors were opened. Gunner was ushered into an animal crate and loaded onto the van.

"Something tells me, this is not going to be fun," he thought as the van started on its journey.

Sensing safety, the five dogs crawled out from under the porch and chased the white van back down the driveway, all the way to the edge of the farm.

BARK!

WOOF!

The van had no windows, so Gunner had no idea where he was going or why. It didn't take long for nearly all of the strange dogs to settle down, and there was not much to do but sleep, which suited him fine.

As he slept, Gunner dreamt about where he could be headed and what might await him. The farm was nice, but there were...

no fun, energetic children to play with,

no toys to call his own, since five dogs claimed ownership, and

no cool, fresh water to swim in; only a stinky mud puddle behind the barn.

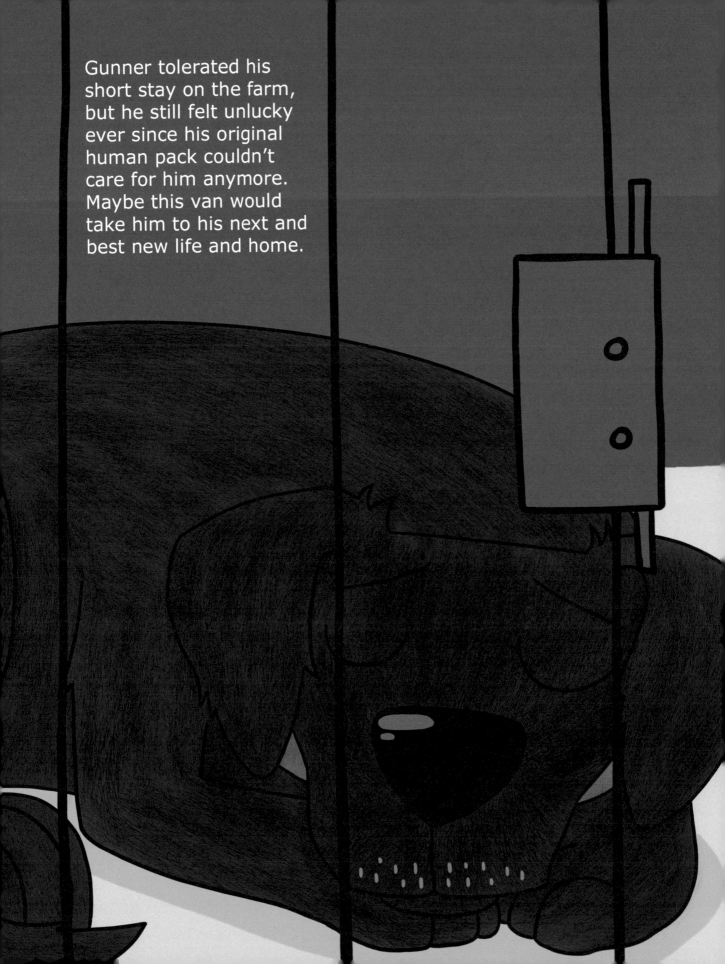

Gunner tolerated his short stay on the farm, but he still felt unlucky ever since his original human pack couldn't care for him anymore. Maybe this van would take him to his next and best new life and home.

For what seemed like days, the van rumbled on, and the other dogs whispered rumors that the destination was Florida.

Gunner could only continue to dream...

about how he might win the state dog
show and appear on the red carpet,

or how he might win a million dog bones in the Doggo Lottery,

or how he would be MVP at this year's Dog Bowl Championship game.

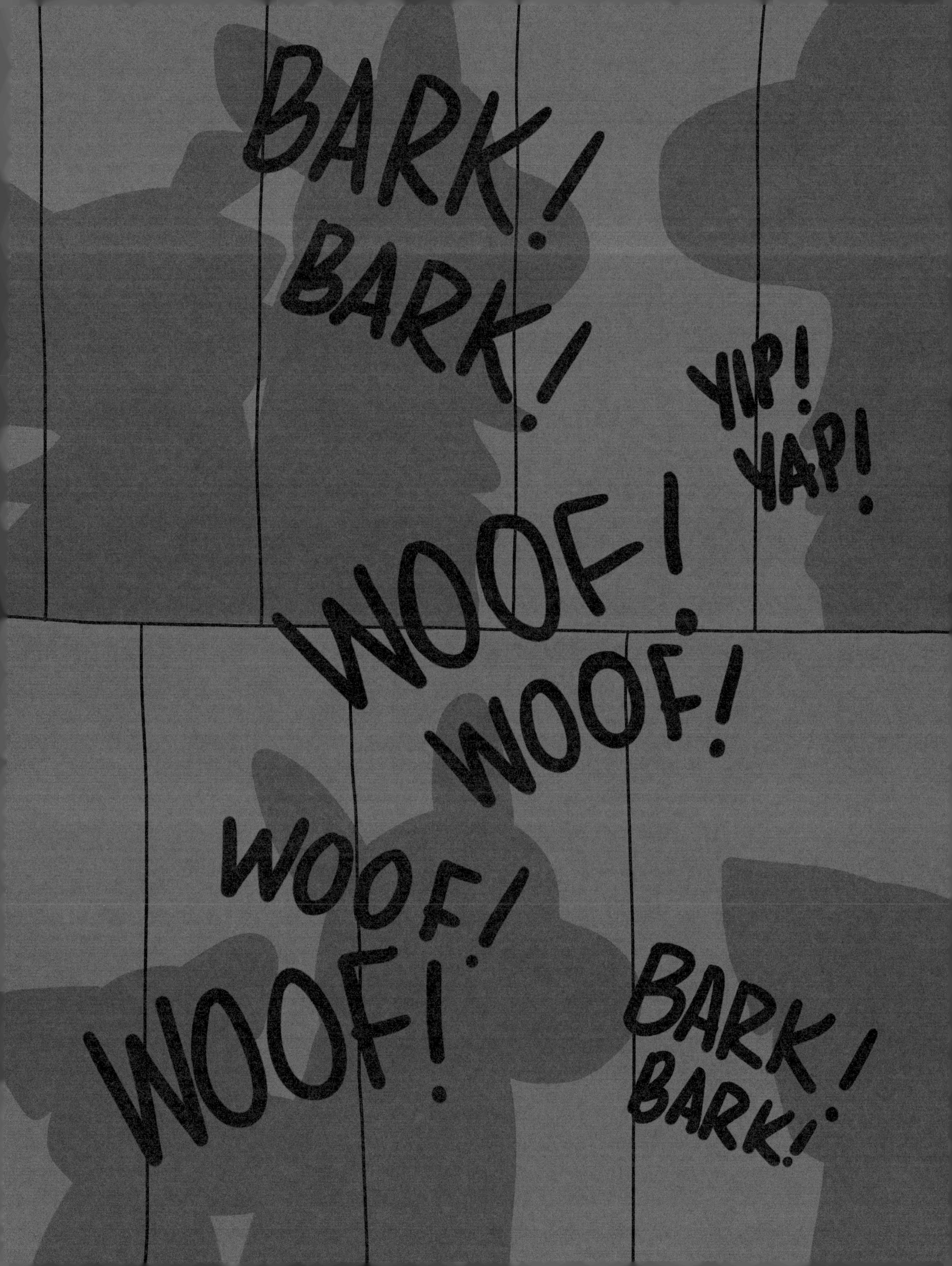
BARK! BARK!
YIP! YAP!
WOOF!
WOOF!
WOOF!
WOOF!
BARK! BARK!

A nice woman called out to the driver man, "That's him... that's Gunner!" Gunner was pleased to hear his name, which likely meant that was his stop. Trying to stay positive, he wagged his tail and perked-up his ears.

Leaping out of the van and into the back of a clean car, Gunner already felt better. This car had windows, and he could look out! This car didn't have 25 or so noisy dogs and it was blissfully quiet.

As the woman drove, Gunner saw through the windows some dairy cows grazing in a field,

a pond, with some sunbathing ducks,
that didn't seem smelly,

and a rather confident dog taking his human
for a walk. "So far, so good," thought Gunner.

As they turned the last corner and into a driveway, Gunner's excitement grew and grew. Would it be all he had hoped and dreamed about?

A eight-year-old boy raced out the front door towards the car as Gunner thought to himself, "Oh, yeah! That's a good sign!"

The boy led Gunner into the house where he saw a nice comfy dog bed AND an oversized dog toy bin packed full of brand-new toys.

Gunner thought, "This has really started out well," and almost pinched himself.

And that's when he saw it...
in the backyard... Gunner's
own swimming pool!!
"BINGO!!", Gunner thought
to himself as he realized he had
just won the Doggo Lottery!

That night, feeling lucky and grateful knowing he was in his "furever" new home, Gunner lay down on his new comfy dog bed. He began to dream about his next adventure...

Behind every lucky dog is an equally as lucky family.

Gunner is a 9-year-old Black Labrador Retriever who came to our family as a foster via Florida All-Retriever Rescue (FARR) in 2019. While the placement was intended as only temporary, Gunner successfully made our foster house his "furever" home and he has been a part of our family ever since. He loves to play fetch and swim (like it's nobody's business), understands a LOT of human words, tucks his boy into bed every night, and is always up for a car ride, but his favorite rides include grabbing a "pup-cup" at Twistee Treat!

About the author:

From first-time author, Karl Riemensperger, comes Gunner Gets Lucky! Karl is a U.S. Marine veteran married to his wife Karen since 2009. Together, they have shared a special love for the Labrador Retriever breed, and often volunteer their home as respite for dogs needing help finding a home. Their daily lives and adventures with Gunner are the inspiration for the books; Gunner was special and wanted to share his story with the world while also supporting rescues who are often in very dire financial straits. Karl quickly got to work writing the first of the series, but the stories didn't stop there and before they knew it, one book became four and more! Having raised five children, Karl considers himself an expert in reading bedtime stories to children, with lots of practice over the years. Karl wrote the books in this series while thinking of the kind of books he enjoyed reading to his children and with the humor of the child and parent in mind.

Made in the USA
Columbia, SC
03 December 2024

47189524R00020